Wilbie's Gift

For my husband

First published in Great Britain in 2006
by Piccadilly Press Ltd,
5 Castle Road, London NW1 8PR

Text and illustration copyright © Sally Chambers, 2006

Text designed by Louise Millar
Colour reproductions by Dot Gradations Ltd, UK
Printed and bound by WKT in China

ISBNs: 1 85340 824 7 (hardback)
1 85340 819 0 (paperback)

EANs: 9 781853 408243 (hardback)
9 781853 408199 (paperback)

1 3 5 7 9 10 8 6 4 2

A catalogue record of this book is available from the British Library

Other titles in the series:
WILBIE – FOOTIE MAD!
WILBIE FINDS A FRIEND
WILBIE AND HARRY

Sally Chambers lives in Hayes, Kent.
She has written and illustrated a number of picture books,
including the titles in the WILBIE series and the TOFFEE series.

Wilbie's Gift

Sally Chambers

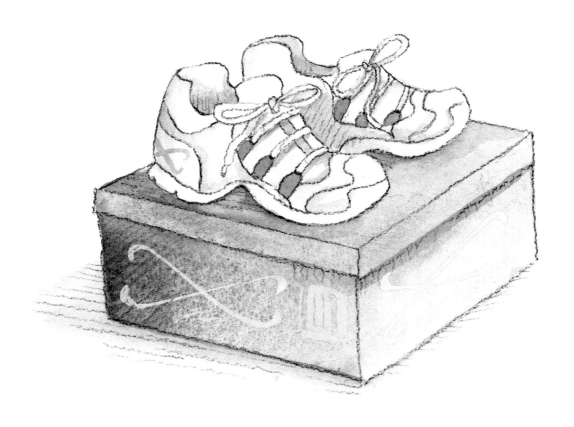

Piccadilly Press • London

Wilbie and Harry were walking home from school one day when Wilbie suddenly stopped in front of the shoe shop.

There, in the window, were the most fantastic trainers that Wilbie had ever seen! "Wow!" he said. "I *really* want those trainers."

"If I had those trainers," said Wilbie, "I bet I'd win all the races on sports day."

"And you'd always get picked first for football," Harry replied.

"Everyone would be *very* jealous," said Wilbie. Wilbie wanted the trainers so much that he was sure his mum would buy them for him.

Wilbie asked his mum about the trainers at suppertime,
but she told him to eat up and ask her later.

He asked about them at breakfast the next morning,
but the doorbell rang before she could answer.

Wilbie kept trying to ask his mum. At bedtime she said they would talk about them tomorrow.

But Wilbie couldn't wait any longer. He decided to go downstairs and ask his dad instead.

His dad listened carefully. Then he said,
"I'm afraid we can't buy trainers just at the
moment. We need to save our money for
something very important . . ." He smiled.
"You're going to have a baby sister!"

Wilbie was very surprised and very disappointed. His dad saw Wilbie's sad face. "Maybe if you saved all your pocket money and your birthday money you could buy them yourself."

When Wilbie got up the next day he felt very cross.
He'd much rather have new trainers than a sister.

He looked at the trainers on the
way to school and they seemed
even more fantastic than before.
Every time he saw them he
liked them better.

"I really don't want there to be a baby around," Wilbie told Harry. "Especially not a *girl* . . .

She'll make me play
with dolls.

She'll want to watch girls'
television programmes.

Mum will put *pink* icing
on cakes.

And Dad won't have time
to play football with me
any more."

Over the next few weeks everyone was getting ready for the baby.

Wilbie's dad painted the nursery.

His grandma knitted clothes.

His grandad made a toybox.

And his mum sewed curtains.

The baby was going to have lots of new things.
It wasn't fair!

One day Wilbie peeped into
the baby's room. Everything
was ready for her.

But then Wilbie
noticed that something
very important was missing.

Wilbie thought about it
all day. Suddenly he had
an idea . . .

A few days later, Wilbie came home from
school to find his mum wasn't there.

"The baby has arrived!" his grandma called,
rushing in from the garden. "Let's go and meet her!"
Wilbie hurried upstairs to get a parcel from under his bed.

At the hospital his mum gave Wilbie a big hug. Then he looked into the cot. There was the tiniest, most beautiful thing he had ever seen. His baby sister!

Wilbie pulled the parcel
from his bag.

"This is for you," he said
to his sister as he undid
the string.

Inside was a lovely, cuddly
teddy bear. He had
bought it with the
money he'd been
saving for the trainers.

Wibie showed his sister the teddy and he thought she looked very pleased. "What a lovely idea!" said his mum.

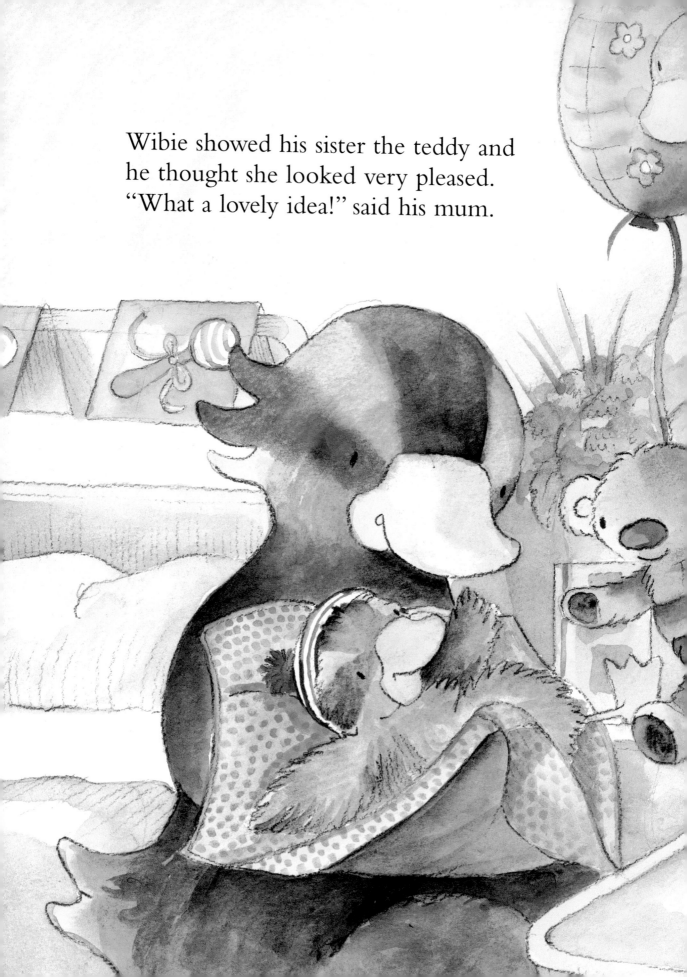

"Well, she *had* to have a teddy,"
said Wilbie.

When his sister came home from hospital, his dad handed Wilbie a box. On the lid was written, "To the best brother in the world!"

Inside were the trainers! Wilbie was delighted.
"Thank you," said Wilbie.

"They're fantastic . . .
And I think my baby sister is fantastic too!"